# Disaster strikes!

Charlie didn't like the look on her mother's face. Mrs. Clark got a certain twinkle in her blue eyes when she was in the grip of some great new idea. Her "great ideas" always involved moving Charlie off the big, comfortable couch, away from the television set, and into some activity that Charlie inevitably despised.

"What do you think of ballet?" Mrs. Clark asked, too casually. Her tone of voice put Charlie on the alert. "I think you'd be terrific at it."

There it was. The "great idea" was out. And it was even more horrible than Charlie had expected.

*No Way Ballet*

# Who Let Those Girls into Ballet Class?

**by Suzanne Weyn**
illustrated by Joel Iskowitz

This edition published in 2001 by Troll Communications L.L.C.

Copyright © 1990 by Troll Communications L.L.C.

Cover photos © Kelly Mooney Photography/CORBIS

ISBN 0-8167-7240-1

Printed in Canada.

10  9  8  7  6  5  4  3  2  1

# One

Charlie Clark stretched out luxuriously on the living room sofa. This was heaven. Friday afternoon and no one was home. Her mother was at the mall, her father still at work, and her three brothers all at football practice. With the remote in her hand, Charlie had complete control of the television. She was queen of the airwaves with no one to disturb her.

Click. Charlie checked in to see how Reva Harris was doing on *Search for Love,* her favorite soap opera. Charlie admired Reva. When she watched the beautiful actress toss her silky black hair over her shoulders and say something witty, Charlie would toss her fine, straight hair and repeat the words Reva said. Somehow they sounded better when Reva said them. It was hard for a ten-year-old girl to sound convincing saying things like, "I've been truly in love with all the men in my life." Still, Charlie liked to dream she was a tall, raven-haired beauty instead of a short, red-haired fifth-grader.

When *Search* had a commercial break, Charlie clicked the remote to watch the game show *Prize Bonana.* "Go for car number three!" she cried, enjoying the way her voice mixed with that of the screaming studio audience. "The magic key is in the backseat of the Passat." But no, the contestant went for the Mustang convertible and lost. Sure enough, the magic key was in the Passat. "I've just got to get on that show," Charlie muttered, imagining herself behind the wheel of a gleaming new car, waving happily to the audience.

Charlie heard the jangle of keys in the front door and quickly switched to one of the educational channels. *Cooking Around the World* was on. A man in a white chef's hat was demonstrating how to wrap a hen in pastry dough. Charlie sat up straight and rested her chin in the palm of her hand, trying to look completely absorbed in the super-boring program.

Charlie's mother stepped into the living room, her arms loaded with packages. She looked at her daughter and sighed. "It's a gorgeous day, Charlie," she said. "The sun is shining, the leaves are starting to turn color. Why don't you go outside and enjoy it?"

"But, Mom, I'm watching educational TV. See?" Charlie protested, pointing to the screen.

Mrs. Clark laughed despite herself. "I'm sure knowing how to wrap a Cornish hen in pastry dough will come in very handy someday," she said.

"You never know, Mom," Charlie said seriously, not taking her eyes from the set.

Mrs. Clark settled on the edge of the big plaid couch and watched the program for a few minutes. "Did they ever find Reva's half-brother?" she asked casually.

Charlie's eyes lit with enthusiasm. "Just today they discovered that Reva's demented twin sister, Alice, kidnapped—" Charlie cut herself short. "That's no fair, Mom."

"Caught you," her mother teased, poking Charlie in the shoulder. "I'm sorry, Charlie, but I can't stand to see my darling daughter turning into a couch potato."

"There's nothing else to do since Karen moved," Charlie argued. Karen was Charlie's best friend, but she had moved to Chicago last summer because her father had been transferred.

"All you and Karen used to do was watch TV together," Mrs. Clark pointed out.

"That's why we were such good friends. Karen really knew how to have fun. She could tune in channels we don't even get."

"I remember. We were all watching Spanish-speaking stations for two days until she came over and readjusted the set."

"She's really talented," Charlie said fondly.

"Yes, well . . . I think it's time you thought about developing some talents of your own," Mrs. Clark said as she rose from the couch and hung her coat in the front-hall closet. Charlie didn't like the look on her mother's face. There was a certain twinkle in her blue eyes that Mrs. Clark got when she was in the grip of some great new idea. Her "great ideas" always involved moving Charlie off the big, comfortable couch, away from the television set, and into some activity that Charlie inevitably despised.

"I have lots of talents, Mom," Charlie insisted, knowing she would have to think and talk fast. "I'm good at . . . English in school, and . . . I was second runner-up in an essay contest last year. My essay was called 'TV, the World's Greatest Invention,' remember?"

Charlie's mother chuckled and settled into the gray overstuffed chair next to the couch. "Yes, you were very convincing. I even remember the last line: 'If the great light of TV is ever turned off, our world will fall into a horrible darkness.'"

Charlie was still very proud of that line and was glad her mother remembered it. She tried to think of some more talents she possessed. *I can play the themes from six different sitcoms on the phone keypad,* she thought, but then decided that might backfire with her mother. She could list every new car that had been advertised on TV in the past three months. But, no, her mother wouldn't be impressed.

"I know you're talented," Mrs. Clark said. "That's exactly why I don't want to see you wasting your potential by sitting in front of the TV."

"You learn a lot of interesting things on TV," Charlie protested. "You learn all about how criminals think, and how police catch them. You get to see how rich and famous people live. I mean, can you really think of a better way for me to spend my time?" Charlie winced; she knew that last sentence had been a mistake. Her mother could *always* think of a better way for her to spend her time. "Better" in her mother's eyes, anyway.

"What do you think of ballet?" Mrs. Clark asked, too casually. Her tone of voice put Charlie on the alert. There was no mistaking it: Mrs. Clark had just come up with another of her "great ideas."

"There's a perfect example," said Charlie in one last, desperate attempt to sidetrack her mother. "Edu ational TV has some great ballets coming up. I hadn't planned to watch them, but if you'd like me to—no problem."

"I was thinking more along the lines of *learning* ballet," her mother said. "I think you'd be terrific at it."

There it was. The "great idea" was out. And it was even more horrible than Charlie had expected. "Ballet?" she shrieked. "Ballet! But, Mom, you know I'm totally uncoordinated. I practically failed gym last year."

"That's all the more reason for you to take ballet lessons," her mother insisted as she leaned forward in her chair. "Besides, everyone in this family is athletic. You're just out of shape because you spend every minute glued to the tube."

"But, Mom . . . but, but . . ." Charlie stammered, jumping to her feet. "It's really not a good time for me. You've been bugging me to clean my room, and I was planning to do it this Saturday—and who knows how long that's going to take. It could take days . . . months. And I have to do a science project for school, and I . . . and I . . ."

"Your room can wait," her mother said. "I'd rather see you take ballet lessons. I'm sure you'll get your science project done, too."

Charlie looked pained. "Do I have to, Mom?"

"I'm going to insist that you at least give it a try. I noticed a cute-looking ballet school today when I was at the Eastbridge Mall, Miss Claudine's School of Ballet. Here." Mrs. Clark reached into her pocket and unfolded a pink piece of paper. "I went in and got a schedule of classes. They've just started. You'll only have missed one or two."

*Cute!* Charlie thought with disbelief. How could any

school be cute? This was awful. It was bad enough that she had to suffer through gym twice a week. Now she was going to have to suffer through ballet classes, too! It was just one more embarrassing opportunity for her to demonstrate to the world that she was totally, hopelessly clumsy.

"But I won't know anybody there," Charlie whined, feeling as if her world was coming to an end.

Mrs. Clark looked thoughtful. "You've just given me a great idea," she said. "At the last PTA meeting some of the parents were looking for activities to involve their children in. I'm going to call the parents on my PTA list and see if there are any who'd like to enroll their kids in ballet class. Maybe we could even carpool. This is going to work out perfectly."

Charlie plopped facedown onto the couch and moaned loudly into the cushions. It kept getting worse and worse. Now that she thought of it, she didn't want anyone she knew to be in her ballet class. All the kids at school would hear how klutzy she was. She could just imagine them calling her "Twinkle Toes Clark" and giggling as she walked down the hall.

"Don't be so melodramatic, Charlie," her mother said. "I think you'll really like ballet. I'm going to make those calls right now. If I can get this organized, we can start you tomorrow in a Saturday beginners' class."

Charlie lifted her head. "Tomorrow!" she wailed. "Isn't that a little sudden?"

"Why wait?" her mother asked cheerily. She gathered her packages and went upstairs, humming a tune from *The Nutcracker* ballet.

Charlie rolled over on the couch and clicked the remote back to *Search for Love*. Reva Harris had failed to rescue her half-brother and was talking to her boyfriend at a café near the ocean. Her long hair was blown back by the breeze as she looked straight into the camera. "Some days start out so well," she said, "and then—*poof*—disaster strikes."

"You can say that again, Reva," Charlie muttered. "You can sure say that again."

At eight-thirty the next morning, Mrs. Clark peeked into Charlie's bedroom. "Let's go, Charlie. We have to be at Miss Claudine's by ten-thirty to register before class, and I have to pick up Emma and Lindsey along the way."

Charlie pulled the covers over her head. "This isn't happening. It's all a dream," she mumbled to herself hopefully. Charlie couldn't believe that her mother had actually convinced Lindsey Munson's father to make his daughter take ballet. Lindsey was in Charlie's class, but they didn't hang around with the same kids. The thing that impressed Charlie most about Lindsey was that Lindsey was actually shorter than she was. Other than lack of height, they had nothing in common. Lindsey was the kind of girl who seemed to Charlie more like a boy. Lindsey lived for playing sports, while Charlie devoted a great deal of time to avoiding physical activity of any kind, so it wasn't strange that the two girls didn't have much to say to each other. Charlie could certainly not picture square-shouldered, boyish Lindsey in a ballet class.

The other girl who had been ensnared in the web of

Mrs. Clark's "great idea" was Emma Guthrie. Emma was new in school, so Charlie didn't know anything about her—except that she struck Charlie as sort of strange. She liked to dress in black and purple and sometimes wore lipstick and mascara to class. No one else in the fifth grade at Eastbridge Elementary wore makeup, and Charlie couldn't think of anyone besides Emma who wore purple and black. Charlie wasn't sure whether Emma was the ballet type or not. It was possible that she was.

"Come on, Charlie," her mother called up the stairs.

Charlie rolled out of bed and went to the top of the stairs. "I don't have any ballet stuff to wear. I can't go."

"It says on the schedule that leotards are provided. Just wear something comfortable."

It was clear to Charlie that there was no getting out of this, so she pulled on her jeans, her big, nubby blue knit sweater, and her new pink high-top sneakers and headed downstairs.

"It's the ballerina!" shouted Charlie's thirteen-year-old brother, Harry, when she was halfway down the stairs. Harry and John, her fifteen-year-old brother, were sitting on the couch watching TV. Even though they were a year and a half apart, everyone always said John and Harry could be twins. They both had the same wavy, reddish-brown hair, freckles, and hazel-colored eyes. This year, though, John had grown to be just under six feet, which made him about four inches taller than Harry.

When they saw Charlie, they leaped to their feet and began spinning around the living room on their toes with their arms held over their heads. The sight of these big spinning hulks might have made Charlie laugh on another day, but today she didn't appreciate the joke.

Charlie stuck her tongue out at them and proceeded down the stairs. They came up behind her, and each boy grabbed hold of her from under her armpits and lifted her into the air.

"Hey, cut it out!" she shouted, swinging her legs wildly, trying to kick her brothers. Laughing and still doing their comical imitation of ballet dancers, Harry and John carried her into the kitchen.

"That's enough," scolded Mrs. Clark, who was sitting at the kitchen table with Mr. Clark and Charlie's oldest brother, Frank. "Sit down and eat these eggs before they get cold."

Charlie pushed her eggs around on her plate as her brothers talked about the big varsity football game coming up between Eastbridge High and Highland Park High. Seventeen-year-old Frank was the captain of the varsity football team, and John was on the team, too. Harry wasn't playing because he was on the junior varsity team, but he was just as excited about the game as his brothers were.

"We're going to cream 'em," Frank was boasting. Charlie rolled her eyes. She would never understand what the big deal was about big guys running up and down a field, holding a ball and trying not to get mowed down by other big guys in football gear. It sounded to Charlie more like a punishment than something you'd actually do for fun.

Charlie looked at her father, who was sitting next to Frank. Harry, John, and she looked like their father. Frank, with his blue eyes and dark brown hair, looked more like their mother. One thing all her brothers and her parents had in common, though, was that they were tall. Charlie couldn't understand how she had turned out to be such a runt in this family of giants. Her mother said she wasn't done growing yet, but, still, she was one of the shortest kids in her class.

"So, you're off to a new adventure this morning, I hear," her father said pleasantly, turning away from the football conversation and toward Charlie.

"Please, I was trying not to think about it," Charlie answered grimly. She knew there was no sense in begging her father to let her stay home. Her parents always stuck together on decisions like this.

"Aw, come on," he coaxed. "It'll be fun."

"Yeah, some fun," Charlie muttered, still pushing her scrambled eggs around on her plate. She didn't feel like eating. Maybe she could say she had lost her appetite because she was sick. No, she had tried that just last week when she wanted to stay home to avoid a physical fitness test at school. Her parents hadn't fallen for it then—and they hadn't even known about the test. Today they would be on the lookout for any tricks like that.

"Come on, Charlie, we'll be late," her mother said all too soon.

"Ta, ta," Harry teased in a silly, high-pitched voice, waving his napkin at Charlie.

"You'll do great, squirt," Frank said kindly.

"Yeah, sure," Charlie mumbled. "And don't call me squirt."

"Knock 'em dead," called her father.

Charlie followed her mother outside and slid into the middle seat of the family's blue minivan. "Let's see now," said Mrs. Clark as she and Charlie fastened their seat belts. "Emma Guthrie lives on Maplewood, number seventy-six. I guess we should pick her up first."

Charlie decided to try one last strategy. "You know, Mom, Emma Guthrie is kind of weird. I'm not sure you want me hanging out with her."

"Her mother sounded perfectly nice on the phone. What's weird about Emma?"

"I can't explain it. You'll see," Charlie said, folding her arms and resigning herself to her horrible fate. Up until now ballet class had seemed the worst of her troubles. Suddenly she felt shy and uncomfortable at the thought of having two girls who she wouldn't ordinarily have had anything to do with sitting right there in her family's van.

Mrs. Clark maneuvered the van through the tree-lined streets of Eastbridge until they came to Maplewood. She pulled into the driveway of a small cedar-shingled house. Immediately the front door of the house opened, and a petite woman with dark, almost black, hair pulled back tightly into a braid waved at them. She disappeared back inside the house and didn't return.

"I wonder what's going on," Mrs. Clark said, looking at her watch.

"I told you she was weird," Charlie reminded her matter-of-factly.

The door flew open again, and Charlie and her mother heard the sound of raised voices coming from the house. "You're going and that's final!" Mrs. Guthrie shouted.

A moment later, Emma appeared on the front steps wearing a purple quilted jacket and black stretch pants. Her long brown hair was pinned up on one side with a bright red plastic clip. Her mother quickly stepped out next to her. Emma glowered at her mother with defiant eyes as Mrs. Guthrie took hold of her daughter's arm and guided her sternly toward the car.

Charlie looked at her mother to gauge her reaction to the scene. Just as she had hoped, her mother's brows were knit, and her lips tightened into a look of anxious disapproval.

When they were just a few feet from the van, Emma suddenly balked and started pulling away. But Mrs. Guthrie had her in an iron grip. No matter how hard Emma pulled, she couldn't escape.

"See what I mean?" Charlie pressed, hoping against hope that her mother would be so appalled by Emma's behavior that she would decide she didn't want Charlie influenced by the girl. "Weird."

"Hmm," her mother muttered absently.

Mrs. Guthrie now held Emma's two arms firmly. They were near enough to the van that Charlie could hear what she was saying.

"Look, Emma, you have everything it takes to be a great dancer," Mrs. Guthrie said in a low, angry voice. "I don't know why you're being so obstinate about this."

"I don't want to be a dancer. I want to be a painter," Emma shouted.

"How do you know what you want to be? You're only ten years old," Mrs. Guthrie snapped. "Besides, you're making a scene in front of these people."

Her mother's last words seemed to make an impression on Emma. She looked quickly over to the van. With an air of wounded pride she straightened her shoulders and said, "All right, Mother, since you don't care how I feel, I suppose I'll have to go." Tossing her head back, like a princess who was suffering a great injustice, she walked toward the van.

Charlie certainly understood how Emma felt, even though she couldn't picture herself behaving like Emma in a million years. Charlie knew her mother would tolerate her acting up like that for about two minutes, and then she would be sent to her room for at least the rest of the day. But, with a sigh, Charlie realized her mother wasn't horrified enough by Emma to forget about ballet.

Emma sat in the backseat. "Hello, Emma," said Mrs. Clark brightly. "I think you know Charlie from school, and I'm Mrs. Clark."

"Pleased to meet you," Emma said with flat primness, not even bothering to acknowledge Charlie's presence.

"I'm sure you'll both really like this class once you get started," Charlie's mother chirped happily.

"I don't think so," said Emma. "I've taken ballet classes before, and I've detested every moment."

Charlie slumped down in her seat and jammed her hands in her jeans pockets. This was going to be a long day.

# Two

"I can't believe this!" cried Mrs. Clark, sticking her head out of the van window to survey the traffic tie-up ahead of her. "If they don't move that stalled car soon, we'll be late."

"No problem, Mom, really," said Charlie.

"We don't mind at all, honestly," insisted Lindsey Munson from the backseat. They had picked up Lindsey after Emma. Though she hadn't thrown a tantrum, as Emma had, it was clear from her grim attitude that she was no more thrilled about being enrolled in Miss Claudine's than Emma and Charlie were. Until now, she had sat with her arms folded tightly and hadn't spoken more than a few tight-lipped hellos.

Lindsey looked at the tangle of traffic ahead of them and then turned to Emma and gave the thumbs-up sign. Emma smiled for the first time since getting into the van. The miracle that she had been praying for was happening—she was going to be spared the unspeakable horror of enrollment in yet another ballet school.

"We might as well just turn back now," Emma said seriously. "If you get a late start, well, you can forget about ever catching up. You're always behind the other students and it's . . . it's a nightmare."

Mrs. Clark turned around and eyed Emma skeptically.

"I don't think being fifteen minutes late will make much difference," she commented flatly.

"You'd be surprised," said Emma. "Timing is everything in ballet."

"There's another thing, Mrs. Clark," Lindsey pressed, wanting to make the most of this possible opportunity. "We're already ten years old. That's way too late to begin ballet lessons. All the great dancers start at four or five. A girl in our class at school has been taking lessons since she was three. She told me that in ballet terms we're practically ancient . . . we're like baseball players who only learned to play when they were twenty or something. I mean, forget it, we're just too old. It's hopeless."

"They're right, Mom," Charlie insisted. "Last year on *Search for Love*, Reva Harris developed amnesia because she flubbed a big ballet audition, and she couldn't bear to live with the shame. Maybe she was late for her first class, or began classes when she was already ten, and her trouble started way back then."

"That's enough," said Mrs. Clark sternly, obviously rattled by the blare of car horns outside and the mutiny she sensed brewing inside the van. "People very rarely develop amnesia in real life, Charlie. It's mostly a TV disease. Did you ever personally know anyone who had amnesia?"

"I wish I had amnesia now so I could forget about ballet," Charlie said sourly.

"Ballet is a beautiful art form and great exercise," Mrs. Clark insisted as she edged the van slowly into the moving traffic in the next lane. "Even if you don't pursue it professionally, ballet develops poise, grace, and good posture. I wish I had taken lessons when I was a girl."

"It's never too late, Mom. You can take the lessons, and we'll just look around the mall."

"Charlie." Her mother's exasperated tone told her to drop the subject.

Charlie turned to face the other girls. Emma was leaning over Lindsey, and both girls were looking out the side window to see what was blocking North Eastbridge Road. In the far lane a dented yellow Chevy was spewing gray-blue smoke from beneath its open hood. The driver, a tall, thin woman wearing a red knit cap and a matching red quilted jacket, paced back and forth. She wrung her hands as she stood helplessly watching the billowing cloud of fumes.

Lindsey nodded at Emma encouragingly. "That car's not going anywhere," she whispered, but when the two girls realized Charlie was looking at them, they stiffened and went back to looking out the window.

Charlie swiveled back around in her seat. She couldn't really blame Emma and Lindsey for being mad at her. After all, it was her mother who had contacted their parents and started this whole mess to begin with. Still, it wasn't really fair of them to be angry at her. Charlie was just as much a victim of her mother's zeal for ballet lessons as they were.

Charlie told herself she didn't like them, either, so it didn't matter, but the unfairness of being blamed for something that wasn't her fault gave her a bad feeling in her stomach. Despite herself, she wanted Emma and

Lindsey to understand that if it were up to her, they would all be home watching Saturday morning TV right now.

"Uh-oh," murmured Emma. Charlie looked out the window and saw a yellow tow truck making its way through the traffic. All too quickly it reached the troubled car. A man jumped out, and in minutes he had the car hooked to the cables of his truck. The tall woman climbed into the truck beside him, talking to the man excitedly, and soon the truck was dragging the car out of the way.

"Thank goodness," sighed Mrs. Clark.

"Ohhhhh," moaned the three girls at once, sinking dejectedly into their seats. The cars began moving again, and it wasn't long before the gleaming, modern stores of the Eastbridge Mall came into view.

Emma stared out the window. She usually enjoyed going to the mall. Ever since she'd moved to Eastbridge from Manhattan last July, after her parents divorced, it was the only thing about Eastbridge she *did* enjoy.

There was a great shop where Emma could buy the dangly Day-Glo earrings she loved, and another one that sold funky T-shirts and leggings. Those were styles Emma felt good wearing—not like the boring crew-neck sweaters and jeans her new classmates at Eastbridge Elementary practically lived in.

Emma sighed to herself as they pulled into the circular road that wrapped around the mall. She knew that these ballet classes would end the same way as the last three times her mother had insisted she try ballet. She would find a zillion ways to avoid class, including getting all the way up to the front door and then bolting. Finally the teacher would get the message that Emma had no intention of becoming a serious ballerina and would request—to Emma's great relief—that she not return.

Emma wished her mother would also get the message. But she never did. Mrs. Guthrie had taken years of lessons and had wanted to be a professional dancer, but she had had Emma instead. So now Mrs. Guthrie was a literary agent, and Emma was supposed to be the dancer.

No matter how much Emma protested, her mother wouldn't listen. "You're thin and graceful like I was at your age," her mother would say. "You were born to dance." Emma didn't agree. Ballet just made her muscles ache and made her feel self-conscious and awkward. And she always seemed to be a step behind everyone else in the class. What made her happy was painting and sketching. She was going to be an artist, not a ballerina.

Mrs. Clark turned into the parking lot. Although it was just after ten in the morning, the lot was filling up quickly because it was Saturday.

"Here we are," Mrs. Clark said as she pulled into a parking space close to the rear entrance of the mall.

"We're here, all right," muttered Charlie, pulling herself out of the middle seat.

Lindsey and Emma slid out of the backseat. Lindsey jammed her hands into the pockets of her jean jacket and scowled. "I'm not wearing one of those tutu things," she growled to no one in particular.

"You wear leotards," Emma informed her. "They don't look too bad."

"Maybe on you they don't," sulked Lindsey, running her

hand through her curly blonde hair. "And they better not ask me to put my hair in a bun or something weird like that, because I won't." She scowled at her reflection in the van window. She couldn't picture her compact square-shaped body in a leotard, spinning gracefully across a stage.

"Look over there," Charlie said. Forgetting to give her the cold shoulder for the moment, Emma and Lindsey looked in the direction she was pointing and saw a tow truck with a dented yellow car attached to its cables. "That's the same car that was holding up traffic on the way over. I wonder what it's doing here."

Emma and Lindsey looked at her and shrugged. Then they remembered they were angry and turned away, acting offended that Charlie had even spoken to them.

They weren't *really* angry at Charlie, but they felt they had to be mad at somebody and they would get in trouble if they were rude to Mrs. Clark. So, without discussing it, they had decided to make Charlie the object of their annoyance over this whole ballet disaster. Even though Emma and Lindsey had just about nothing in common, they were firmly united against their common enemy— Charlie.

"Come on, girls," Mrs. Clark encouraged. "This is going to be fun." The three girls just looked at her as if she was insane and followed sullenly as she led them through the doorway and into the brightly lit mall. Happy music wafted through the air around them. It seemed in sharp contrast to their own gloomy moods.

Lindsey lingered in front of John's Sporting Goods store and examined the goalie's jersey in the front window.

If this ballet stuff interfered with her playing soccer, she vowed, she would never speak to her father again.

Mr. Munson had gotten it into his head that Lindsey should be less of a tomboy and more ladylike the day she had come home with a note from the principal, explaining that his daughter had been fighting with boys in the schoolyard.

The principal's note made it sound much worse than it had been. Lindsey tried to explain to her father that it had all started when they were playing soccer. She was the goalie, and dumb Jonathan Smith kept insisting his goal was good when she had clearly kicked it out. She let it go a couple of times, but by the third time she couldn't listen to him anymore. They argued, she gave Jonathan a little push, and he got all bent out of shape and pushed her back. Then Bob Myers had to get into the act and start shouting. That's when Mrs. Burr, the principal, walked over and blamed the whole stupid thing on Lindsey.

Ever since Lindsey's mother had died two years before, her father had worried that she needed more feminine influences in her life. The note from Mrs. Burr just convinced him he was right. And then, on the very same day, Mrs. Clark called up with the "perfect" solution— ballet lessons. Lindsey almost felt that it was a terrible plot designed to ruin her life, not to mention her chances of playing goalie on the traveling soccer team.

"Come on," Mrs. Clark called. "It's nearly ten-thirty." Lindsey clenched her hands into fists in her pockets, bent her head, and caught up with the others.

They made their way down to the lower level of the

mall. "It figures the school would be down here with all the tacky stores," mumbled Emma as her eye followed the trail of signs: Ernie's Auto Parts; Howard Hardware; Paulsen's Hosiery; The Red Robin Coffee and Donut Shop.

It was easy to spot Miss Claudine's School of Ballet. Not only was the name lettered in large, swirling black script against a pink curtain in the storefront window, but a small sea of about twenty girls with their hair combed up and gathered into topknots stood in front of the door, holding their dance bags and waiting to get in.

Lindsey clutched the sleeve of Emma's jacket. "We've been saved! Miss Claudine's not here!"

# Three

"Guess we'll have to go home," Charlie suggested to her mother as they stood in front of Miss Claudine's and looked at the group of girls waiting for the school to open.

"Let's wait a few minutes and see what happens," Mrs. Clark insisted.

"I'm sure she's not coming, Mom," Charlie argued. "The school's probably out of business already."

Charlie realized that her mother wasn't going to budge, so she wandered over to an appliance store and gazed longingly at the five superwide TV screens that were playing five different stations at once.

Just then a woman came hurrying toward the group at a fast clip. Her red jacket was flying behind her. She pulled off her red hat as she broke into a run, sending her long ash-blonde hair tumbling down to her waist.

*"Pardonnez-moi, mesdemoiselles,"* the woman cried. *"Pardonnez-moi!"* The woman scurried to the front door of Miss Claudine's and whipped a ring of clattering keys from her large black satchel. *"Voilà!"* she exclaimed, unlocking the door and flinging it open dramatically.

"Hey, that's the woman with the broken-down car," Lindsey said to Emma. "She must have talked the tow-truck guy into driving her here."

"How could she talk him into anything?" Emma remarked. "She doesn't even speak English."

"Do you think that's Miss Claudine, herself?" asked Charlie, who had broken away from the bliss of the appliance store and rejoined Emma and Lindsey when the woman appeared. "She seems kind of nutty to me."

Emma and Lindsey nodded, forgetting again to snub Charlie. "She sure does," Lindsey agreed.

"She probably escaped from a French lunatic asylum," offered Emma dramatically.

"Mom, do you think it's safe to leave us here with her?" Charlie asked her mother. "What if one of us gets injured, and she can't call the hospital because she can't speak English? It could be a tragedy. That happened on *The Spinning World* when Rex was hurt on the island of Hunjuju, and the people only spoke Hunjujuan."

"Let's go," said Mrs. Clark, ignoring her daughter's plea. Charlie noticed that though her mother's voice was firm, she looked skeptical. Surely, Charlie reasoned with some hope, she had to realize that Miss Claudine was a little on the eccentric side.

Inside the studio, things were a whirl of activity. Girls ran in and out of a door that obviously led to the dressing room in search of pins, ribbons, and forgotten tights. Miss Claudine seemed oblivious to the chaos around her as she sat serenely behind a large, worn-looking desk, writing in an oversized notebook. Charlie surveyed the room. Behind Miss Claudine to the right was a door with a frosted glass panel that had the word *Office* written on it. Above Miss Claudine's head was a framed photo of a young woman wearing tap shoes, a leotard with a tuxedo jacket, and a plumed hat. There was an inscription on the photo that Charlie couldn't read. She assumed it was one of Miss Claudine's friends or former students.

"Excuse me," Mrs. Clark said, stepping forward.

Miss Claudine looked up from her book. She seemed startled at first but quickly focused on the newcomers. *"Bonjour, mesdemoiselles, madame,"* she greeted them as she rose majestically from behind the desk with her arms outstretched in a welcoming gesture. The three girls instinctively took a step backward, half afraid she was going to gather them together in an embrace.

None of them had ever seen anyone like Miss Claudine. She seemed neither young nor old. They certainly couldn't picture her being anyone's mother. She had pale skin, and her nose and chin were somewhat pointy. She wasn't exactly pretty, but her blue eyes seemed to shine, and her long ash-blonde hair swirled around her shoulders when she spoke. She was tall and thin and wore a lavender leotard, over which she had wrapped a calf-length dance skirt of the same color. "Have you come to register for classes?" she asked.

"Thank goodness," whispered Charlie under her breath, relieved that Miss Claudine spoke at least a few words of English.

Mrs. Clark told Miss Claudine that they had come to register. The teacher filled out a form for each girl, then recorded the checks Mrs. Clark gave her in her big notebook.

Miss Claudine walked around the girls three times with her arms folded, looking them over.

"Mesdemoiselles Emma, Lindsey, and Charlotte," she mused in a melodic voice, as if entering each of their names in her memory.

"I hate the name Charlotte," protested Charlie, wincing at the sound of the name she had been given in honor of her great-grandmother. Her mother frowned at her, so she added more politely, "Please call me Charlie."

"*Non, non, ma chérie*," said Miss Claudine. "Charlotte is a beautiful name. It's French. A beautiful name from the richest language in the world."

"My name is Charlie," Charlie insisted through clenched teeth.

"I cannot have such a name for one of my ballerinas," Miss Claudine objected pleasantly. "I will have to call you Mademoiselle Clark until you come to appreciate the elegance of your true name. Perhaps studying ballet will open your eyes to the Charlotte hiding within you."

Charlie looked to her mother for help, but Mrs. Clark simply winked at her daughter with eyes full of laughter. It was clear to Charlie that her mother was not sympathetic. The graceful dance teacher had won her over already.

"Miss Claudine," called a slim, pretty girl of about eleven or twelve. Her dark hair was drawn up in a sleek bun. "I think we're ready." The girl's gaze fell on Charlie, Emma, and Lindsey. She tilted her head back and narrowed her eyes as she looked at them. Her expression made them feel as if they were mangy dogs who had somehow wandered into the studio. They glared back at her with equal dislike.

"*Merci*, Danielle," Miss Claudine answered the girl. "We will begin momentarily."

Miss Claudine reached into a closet by the front door and pulled out three plastic-wrapped packages containing powder-blue leotards with matching tights and three pairs of soft pink ballet slippers.

"These are included in your fee," Miss Claudine assured Mrs. Clark, who now looked ready to leave. "Class lasts until twelve forty-five. That gives us an hour for ballet and forty-five minutes for my specialty—ballet culture."

*Ballet culture?* thought Charlie with alarm. But she never even got a chance to ask what that was.

"I'll pick you up at one," Mrs. Clark told the girls as she headed for the door. "Have fun."

"Thanks, Mom," said Charlie flatly. "Thanks loads." Annoyed as Charlie was with her mother, she didn't want to see her leave. It was as if her mother was her last link with civilization. Now she was alone in this strange studio with two hostile classmates and . . . Miss Claudine.

Lindsey opened her package and held the leotard out in front of her by two fingers, as if it was a wet rat. "This is baby blue," she said, disgusted by the dainty color. "I thought we'd wear black."

Miss Claudine ignored her comment. Instead she grabbed Lindsey's outstretched arm. "*C'est bon*," she gasped. "Very good! You have a natural reach." Lindsey looked around for a way to escape Miss Claudine's grasp, but the teacher didn't let go.

"Attention, class," Miss Claudine called, gathering the girls around her. "I want you to look at our new student,

*32*

Mademoiselle Lindsey. This is the type of full reach I will be encouraging you to develop. I can tell that Mademoiselle Lindsey will quickly develop a lovely *port de bras*."

Lindsey's eyes went wide in horror, and she felt the heat of a blush rushing to her face. How could Miss Claudine make such a mortifying comment about her bra size—and in front of all these strangers! Lindsey didn't even wear a bra! This woman really was some kind of kook. She pulled away from Miss Claudine and crossed both arms over her chest.

Emma looked at Lindsey's stunned expression and then at Charlie's horrified one. "She just means you hold your arms gracefully," she whispered to Lindsey. "It's ballet talk."

Miss Claudine clapped her hands, and her students scampered into the large mirrored studio behind them. "Danielle, show the *demoiselles* to the dressing room, where they will put on their leotards and slippers," she said.

"Follow me," Danielle ordered haughtily, leading them to the room they had seen the other ballet students dashing in and out of earlier.

Inside the small dressing room the girls changed into their leotards. Charlie felt weird taking off her clothes in front of strangers, especially strangers who weren't exactly being friendly to her. She put the tights on first and then pulled the leotard up under her shirt before taking it off. Standing on tiptoes, she checked herself in the small mirror. She decided it could have been worse; she didn't look that bad.

Emma changed quickly, paying no attention to anyone, and then leaned against the wall with her arms folded in disgust as she waited for the others. After a few seconds, she reached into her bag and pulled out a tube of thick black mascara and began applying it.

Lindsey changed slowly, facing the wall. When she had her leotard and tights on, she glanced quickly in the mirror. Her broad, square shoulders and straight hips looked all wrong to her in this feminine outfit. And the *port de bras* incident had made her doubly self-conscious. She was sure everyone would take one look at her and start laughing.

Lindsey was desperate. How could she go out there looking and feeling so dumb? Then she spotted the long red Yankees T-shirt she had been wearing and quickly slipped it on over the leotard. It fell just past her hips. She looked in the mirror again and decided that with her T-shirt on she could live with the leotard and tights.

"You can't wear that," said Danielle, pointing at Lindsey's T-shirt. "Miss Claudine has to be able to see if your placement is correct."

"My placement is just fine, thanks," snapped Lindsey, not having the faintest idea what Danielle was talking about.

Danielle placed her hands on her hips and stood in front of the doorway. "You're not wearing that T-shirt. Take it off."

"No way," growled Lindsey, facing Danielle nose to nose.

"Miss Claudine!" yelled Danielle. "Oh, Miss Claudine!"

Miss Claudine appeared in the doorway behind Danielle. "*Mesdemoiselles*, what is the problem?" she asked with genuine concern.

"She insists on wearing this ridiculous baseball T-shirt over her leotard, Miss Claudine," Danielle said shrilly. "I told her she had to take it off."

"Who died and put you in charge of the world?" Emma snapped at the girl. Danielle narrowed her eyes and smirked back at Emma.

"I don't see what difference it makes." Charlie spoke up, not wanting to look like a wimp in front of Emma and Lindsey.

"Of course you don't," Danielle said in a superior tone. "You clearly don't know the first thing about the dance." Charlie certainly couldn't argue with that.

"*Merci*, Danielle, I will settle this," said Miss Claudine. "Now be a dear and go get the class warmed up. I will be there in a minute."

"I'd be glad to, Miss Claudine." Danielle threw the girls an I-told-you-so look and swirled out of the room.

Miss Claudine put her graceful hand on Lindsey's shoulder. "You must understand, *chérie,* that I have to be able to see if you are positioning your body correctly. Otherwise, you might injure yourself. It is hard for me to see if you are executing the moves correctly when you are hidden under that big shirt."

Lindsey folded her arms tightly. "I'm not going out there without my T-shirt," she said sulkily. "I'm just not. That's all."

Miss Claudine stepped back and studied Lindsey. "Such

a strong, sturdy body—you should be proud to show it off."

Lindsey just stood with her arms folded, looking at the floor. Part of her wanted to be agreeable, but a bigger part felt too embarrassed to be seen in such a dumb outfit.

Miss Claudine shook her head with a resigned air. "Very well, one step at a time," she said with a deep sigh. "Wear the shirt. If that's what it takes to get you started in your love for the ballet, then it doesn't pay for me to be rigid. Ballet dancers are like flowers. Each has her own gift, but each must unfold, petal by petal, and bloom in her own time."

With a sweep of her arm, Miss Claudine beckoned them to follow. "Come, the dance awaits," she said simply, then turned and walked toward the ballet studio, not bothering to notice whether or not they were with her.

Charlie was the first to follow along behind Miss Claudine. She took her place at the barre, facing the front wall. Danielle was leading the class through a series of what looked to Charlie like painful deep-knee bends. The girls beside her seemed to rise and descend effortlessly. Charlie concentrated on Danielle and tried to follow her every move. It seemed that Miss Claudine expected them to pick up the steps on their own, by watching.

"Backs straight, heads held high," Miss Claudine encouraged them, relieving Danielle of her role as instructor. "When you plié, pretend there is an invisible string attached to your head, and it is pulling you to the ceiling."

Lindsey had taken a spot several girls away from

Charlie, next to the door. She tried to copy the elegant movement, but she did it too rapidly, as if she were in gym class. She definitely didn't have Danielle's flowing grace. This was turning out to be as horrible as she had expected.

Seeking out a sympathetic face, Lindsey looked over her shoulder. She had thought Emma was right behind her, but now she didn't see her anywhere. *Strange*, she thought.

Suddenly Lindsey heard a *pssst* sound. She turned in the direction of the door. At first she didn't see anyone, but then she spotted Emma peeking around the corner. Lindsey realized that Emma had changed back into her clothes.

She shot the other girl a questioning glance, but just then Emma ducked back behind the door. Lindsey looked to Miss Claudine, but the ballet teacher was now bending and rising along with the class.

Lindsey turned toward the doorway again. Emma's head darted out and then back. All Lindsey saw after that was Emma's small hand as she stuck it into the doorway and waved good-bye.

Lindsey couldn't believe it. Emma was cutting ballet class!

# *Four*

Lindsey looked quickly around the studio. Miss Claudine was busy repositioning the feet of a girl at the far end of the room.

She glanced back at the empty doorway where Emma had been standing a second ago. If Emma wasn't staying in class, why should she? She thought of signaling Charlie but then decided against it. She wasn't sure if Charlie would come with her or rat on her. Besides, the two of them wouldn't be able to get out unnoticed.

With another quick check over her shoulder, Lindsey slipped out of the studio to the front room. She caught sight of Emma's purple jacket through the glass of the front door as it closed softly behind her.

Lindsey didn't know what to do. She wanted to change into her regular clothes, but there was no time. If she didn't leave now she'd lose track of Emma, and wandering around the mall by herself didn't seem like much fun to Lindsey.

There was no time for indecision. Miss Claudine might realize she was gone any minute and come looking for her. It was now or never.

Lindsey heard the sound of someone putting on a classical music CD, and then Miss Claudine began to speak. "Danielle will now perform the role of the dying princess from *Swan Lake* for us," she began. "I have rechoreographed the ballet so that none of it is danced *en pointe*. Young ankles can't take the strain of toe dancing. At this year's recital, many of you will play the parts of her swan attendants."

That was all it took to send Lindsey sprinting out the front door. No way was she dancing around Danielle like a love-starved puppy. "Emma, wait up," she called to the girl who was walking quickly away from Miss Claudine's.

Emma whirled around and looked at Lindsey with a panicked expression. Instead of stopping, she began walking even faster.

"Hold on," called Lindsey, running after her.

Emma broke into a run, but Lindsey caught up to her easily. "I'm not going back. Don't try to make me," Emma snapped when Lindsey was alongside her.

"Are you crazy? I don't want to go back. I'm busting out with you," Lindsey explained.

Emma paused and caught her breath as she studied Lindsey suspiciously. "Aren't you afraid of getting in trouble?"

"I don't know. Are you?"

Emma shrugged. "I'm always in trouble. It sort of doesn't bother me anymore. It seems to me that you have two choices: either be in trouble all the time, or always do what other people want you to do. I'd rather be in trouble."

Lindsey had to think about that one. In all honesty, she hated being in trouble. The thought of it usually made her sick to her stomach. She'd never met anyone who didn't care. Most kids she knew did everything in their power to avoid getting into trouble.

Lindsey wondered if Emma was what her father would call a "bad influence," because right now Lindsey didn't care about getting into trouble, either. Something about Emma made her feel that skipping ballet class wasn't anything to worry about.

"I guess I'd rather get into trouble than take that stupid class," she admitted.

Emma smiled, and Lindsey noticed that she looked very different when she wasn't wearing her sour, serious expression—pretty, even. "Do you *believe* that Danielle character? What a jerk!" Emma said.

"'Yes, Miss Claudine. No, Miss Claudine,'" Lindsey mimicked Danielle in a high squeal. Emma laughed, and Lindsey laughed along with her. It suddenly seemed to them as if Miss Claudine's was a terrible experience that was now safely behind them, and it was okay to joke about it.

They strolled through the mall with the delicious feeling of being on a great adventure. It was as if the mall was some strange new land full of fascinating things to explore. They had the feeling that anything could happen.

Emma stopped and breathed deeply. "A mall is really a wonderful place," she said happily. "You could almost live here. Think of it. There are all kinds of food stands with the best foods—hot dogs, French fries, pizza, ice cream. And the big stores, like Horner's, have almost everything else you need. You can watch TV in the electronics department. You can try on expensive stuff, like dresses

*41*

you could never afford to buy. There are puppies and kittens in the pet department. It's almost like having a private zoo. And there's always stuff going on, like fashion shows, concerts, and contests."

The idea of living in a mall suddenly struck Emma as the most wonderful fantasy in the world. No rules, no school, and—as long as she was careful to avoid a certain part of the mall—no ballet class. "You could probably even sleep in those big fancy beds in the furniture department."

Lindsey wasn't so sure. "I think the store has security guards, but maybe you could if you hid under the bed when they made their rounds. You wouldn't get much sleep, though, if you had to keep jumping under the bed, and if you did fall asleep, then you'd get caught."

"Oh, I'd be able to figure something out," said Emma, not wanting a troublesome detail like security guards to spoil her fantasy. She could actually picture herself lounging in one of those big canopy beds in Horner's furniture department. Or maybe she'd rather sink into a bed with a zebra-print headboard. That was the beauty of living in a mall—you could try out a different bed every night.

"Malls are the one thing I like about Eastbridge," she confided to Lindsey. "I can find all the things I love, and the stores remind me of when I lived in Manhattan."

"How come you moved?" asked Lindsey.

"Parents divorced," Emma answered matter-of-factly. "Dad stayed in the city, so I still go in to see him a lot. I'm moving back to the city as soon as I turn eighteen. That's where I really belong."

Lindsey thought for a moment, then decided Emma was right; she did seem more like a city kid. She certainly wasn't like any of the other kids Lindsey knew at Eastbridge Elementary. She seemed older, somehow. The makeup and clothes she wore even made her *look* older.

"I think I belong right here," Lindsey said, "or maybe on a horse ranch. When my mother was alive, we went to a horse ranch in Texas for a week, and I could definitely see myself living there. All we did all day was take care of the horses and ride them around on the trails. I rode a little pony named Scamp. It was wonderful. I've only been to Manhattan once, but it seemed pretty crowded and dirty to me."

"Lots of people think that," Emma said lightly, not offended. She was proud of the fact that not everyone liked the city. Her father said it took a special kind of person to appreciate its pace. "You *are* more the outdoors type," she added, "though you sure don't look it in that getup."

Lindsey stared at her reflection in a store window, suddenly remembering that she was wearing a T-shirt, tights, and ballet slippers. "Do I look too weird? I mean, I won't get arrested or anything, will I?"

"Nah, nobody's even paying attention to us," Emma said. "The T-shirt makes the outfit kind of cool."

"I feel like a giant tooth fairy," Lindsey complained.

That made Emma laugh. "Don't worry, the T-shirt really helps," she assured her.

Lindsey wasn't the kind of girl Emma usually liked. In fact, she had always detested jocks. It seemed to Emma that most jocks tried to make you feel like a wimp just because you weren't interested in sports. But somehow Lindsey was different. She just was who she was, and she didn't seem to be judging Emma for being different. And if there was one thing Emma hated more than anything else in the world, it was being judged.

Emma was glad Lindsey had followed her out of Miss Claudine's. It would have been kind of depressing to roam around the mall all by herself. She would probably have spent the whole time thinking about how much she hated ballet and about how all her other ballet classes had been such disasters. The teachers and students had judged everything about her every second: the way she stood, the way she moved, even the way she held her hands. It was just a festival of being picked apart by strangers. Who needed it?

Emma was suddenly seized by the urge to do something nice for Lindsey. She studied Lindsey's pale, lightly freckled face. "You know what you need?" she said finally.

"What?"

"Makeup."

"Oh, gee, thanks a lot," Lindsey said sarcastically. "Maybe I should just wear a mask. Would that make you happy?"

"Don't get insulted. I didn't mean it that way," Emma explained. "Just about everyone looks better with makeup. I know I do."

Lindsey considered the thick clumps of mascara on Emma's eyelashes. Emma's greenish eyes did appear brighter than they had before she framed them with the mascara. "Maybe it looks okay on you, but it would just look weird on me. Besides, my father would kill me if he saw me with makeup."

"My mother doesn't let me wear makeup, either. That's why I carry it with me in my bag."

"What about when you get home?" Lindsey asked.

"I just wash it off before I go home," Emma explained. "Simple."

Lindsey sighed. "I wouldn't even know how to put it on, anyway."

"That's what I'm here for," said Emma grandly, "to show you. Being in a mall is like being in makeup heaven. Samples of every makeup you can possibly think of are here. There's a great Sparkle Glow counter upstairs at Nevins Department Store. I go there all the time."

Normally Lindsey would have thought it a lot more fun to browse through the sporting goods departments of the big stores, but she knew Emma would never be interested. Besides, it seemed like part of this strange adventure to do something different.

"What the heck," she said. "We have almost two hours to kill until Mrs. Clark picks us up, anyway. . . . Hey, what are we going to do when class is over?"

Emma shrugged. "I guess we can go back to Miss Claudine's and stand out front and act like we've been inside the whole time."

"Do you think Charlie will tell on us?" Lindsey wondered aloud, letting a twinge of her old fear of getting into trouble creep back in.

"You mean 'Mademoiselle Charlotte'?" Emma giggled. "I don't know. She might. I can't really tell."

"I can't tell, either," Lindsey agreed. "I don't know Charlie too well, even though she's been in my class for the past two years. I feel kind of bad. We were pretty mean to her."

"Are you kidding?" Emma protested indignantly. "This whole mess is her fault."

"Come on, Emma, you can't honestly say that. I mean, what was she supposed to do if her mother forced her to take ballet lessons? It's not like she begged to be enrolled at Miss Claudine's and insisted we come with her."

"Then whose fault is it?" Emma asked.

"I guess it's her mother's fault," Lindsey replied thoughtfully. "And our parents' fault. They could have said no when Mrs. Clark called up."

"That's what really bugs me about parents," Emma confessed. "They're always acting like they know what's best for you. When I said I didn't want to take ballet lessons, my mother should have just said, 'Okay, fine.'"

"I know, but sometimes they do know more than we do," Lindsey said.

Emma looked at her as if she was insane. "If my parents know so much, how come they got divorced?" she challenged. "That was a pretty dumb move, if you ask me."

Not waiting for Lindsey to respond, Emma ran over to a poster store and began looking at the pictures in the window. Lindsey followed, and they stood for a while, staring at the posters without talking.

Lindsey thought she knew how Emma felt. She remembered how she had felt two years earlier when her mother died of cancer. Besides the sadness, it was the first time it had occurred to her that her father didn't have the answer to every single one of life's problems. She knew now that it had been babyish to expect him to be able to solve a problem the doctors couldn't solve. Still, at the time, it frightened her that her father was powerless to stop her mother from dying. It was scary to think of her parents as people who didn't have all the answers.

"Stuff happens," Lindsey finally said, "stuff even parents don't know how to fix."

"That's what I'm saying," Emma insisted. "If they don't know everything, they shouldn't go around acting like they do."

Lindsey didn't know how to argue that point, but she wasn't comfortable with the idea. Despite the fact that her father wasn't perfect, she liked believing that he knew a little more than she did. It gave her a safe feeling to think that the adults around her had a pretty good idea of what life was about. And in her heart she was convinced that, in general, they did.

Emma and Lindsey left the poster store and continued walking until they stood in front of the entrance to Nevins. "The Sparkle Glow counter is on the second floor. Come on, you'll love it," said Emma eagerly.

Lindsey was once again filled with a great sense of freedom. "Boy, am I glad we decided to ditch that class. This is fun."

"Yeah," Emma agreed. "I wonder what poor Charlie is doing now."

# *Five*

Charlie watched as Danielle fluttered to the floor and died. The class applauded politely. "*C'est bon*, Danielle," Miss Claudine praised, "very good. You were a bit unsure of yourself in some parts, but you've just learned the dance. With more practice you will be a very beautiful swan princess, indeed."

Danielle rose to her feet and smiled at Miss Claudine. Charlie had to admit she was impressed. Danielle was a graceful dancer, even if she did always wear an unbearable look of superiority on her face.

"Arabesques now, *mesdemoiselles*," said Miss Claudine. She stood in front of the class and extended her leg gracefully into the air behind her. With one flowing movement, her left arm floated up in front of her and her right, behind. The expression on her face was that of calm concentration. She looked to Charlie like a lovely statue.

The girls in the class followed Miss Claudine's example, except that they steadied themselves with one hand at the barre. Though extended legs jutted out at odd angles, Charlie noticed they all managed to stay balanced.

She leaned forward and tried the arabesque. Her standing leg shook uncontrollably as she tried to lift the other one off the ground. Every time her back foot rose more than two inches, she would start to lose her balance

and would have to put it down. No one, not even Miss Claudine, seemed to notice.

*This is the story of my life,* Charlie thought as she wobbled uncontrollably on her one foot; she was the klutziest kid she knew. Her brothers played every sport at school, and they were good at all of them. Her parents played tennis every Saturday, and they were always the ones who organized a volleyball game in the summer or the annual neighborhood touch-football match in the fall.

Even though she resembled her father, it had occurred to Charlie that maybe she had been adopted. How else could she explain the fact that she was so completely different from the rest of her family? She couldn't dribble a basketball, hit a baseball, or kick a soccer ball. And it wasn't that she hadn't tried. Her mother had forced her to try out for every after-school team and league she could find. Mrs. Clark's attempts to separate Charlie from her beloved TV set hadn't begun with ballet. Ballet was just the latest in an endless series of group activities in which Mrs. Clark had wanted her daughter to become involved.

Luckily for Charlie, she never got past the tryout stage in sports. Once the humiliation of striking out, or having to chase a rolling basketball across the court, or whatever, was over, the coach would politely tell her that she hadn't made the team and she could return to the fun of watching TV. But now, with ballet, there were no tryouts, no team to be rejected from. She would just have to be terrible at it and continue to be terrible forever. The thought made Charlie's leg shake even harder.

Miss Claudine had been holding her arabesque. Now

she flowed effortlessly out of the position and the class followed. *Thank goodness that's over,* thought Charlie. She looked behind her to see how Lindsey and Emma were doing.

It was then she realized they were gone!

A cold chill of panic ran up Charlie's spine. She had assumed they were right there in the studio with her all this time. She looked around the room again to be sure. No, they were definitely not there.

Charlie's mind raced wildly. How did they get out? Where could they have gone? What would her mother say when she came to pick them up?

"And again, arabesques," said Miss Claudine, "but this time we will concentrate on balance. I want you all to step away from the barre, toward the center of the room."

The girls spaced themselves out evenly throughout the room and followed Miss Claudine in doing a freestanding arabesque. Not knowing what else to do, Charlie tried the arabesque again, but this time more than just her leg was shaking. She was shaking all over. She lifted her back leg and quickly put it down. She tried again, and this time she stuck her arms out to her sides and flapped them around in a determined attempt to balance herself.

"Shoulders down, heads up high," Miss Claudine coached as she surveyed her class from her arabesque position. "You are all swans, beautiful, graceful swans."

Charlie couldn't think of herself as a swan. She had too much else on her mind—like what she was going to do about the missing Lindsey and Emma. Her mother would kill her. Even though it wasn't her fault, Charlie knew that her mother would blame her for letting them escape. She had to find the girls and get them back to Miss Claudine's before her mother returned to the mall to pick them up.

But how? It was hard to come up with a plan while trying to lift one foot in the air. Feebly, she managed to stand with her back leg bent and lifted slightly behind her. She knew she didn't look too graceful, but she couldn't worry about it now. She had to find a way to sneak out of class so she could search for Emma and Lindsey.

She realized Lindsey had been standing closest to the door, and Emma had probably never even come into the studio. That's how they had gotten away so quietly. But Charlie was in the middle of the class. She couldn't just walk out.

She looked at Miss Claudine, who was now intently working out a series of steps by herself in the corner of the room as the girls continued to practice their arabesques. The teacher didn't even realize that Emma and Lindsey were gone. It was as if the minute she stepped into the studio she became completely focused on ballet and nothing else. Besides, she wasn't used to seeing Emma and Lindsey—or Charlie, for that matter—so their absence probably didn't really register with her.

But could Charlie get away with just walking out? Even if she could have, she didn't have the nerve to try. She had to come up with a plan to get out of the studio unnoticed.

She tried to think. What did people do on TV? They created a disturbance. Reva Harris had once started screaming that she saw a ghost when she wanted her boyfriend to be able to sneak away from a supposedly haunted house. While everyone was looking at her, Lance ducked out the back door.

Somehow Charlie didn't think that would translate too well in her situation. If she started screaming, everyone would be staring at her, and she'd hardly be able to sneak away then. Plus, Miss Claudine would tell her mother, and she'd wind up in even worse trouble.

Maybe the trick was to get someone *else* to create a disturbance while she ran away. Since she had no one to help her, the situation felt just about hopeless to Charlie— but suddenly inspiration struck, or rather it popped its head out.

She noticed a small gray mouse behind a loose piece of wallboard in the corner of the studio by the door. Charlie watched as it cautiously began to make its way along the baseboard toward the pink trash can at the other end of the studio. A torn cellophane wrapper still containing bits of an old coffee cake lay next to the can. It was obviously the prize the mouse was after.

The girls were now spread out around the room, stretching. No one seemed to notice the mouse as it stopped every few feet, sniffed, then scurried forward toward the wrapper.

Knowing a good opportunity when she saw it, Charlie tapped the girl next to her. The girl shot her an annoyed glance, but when Charlie pointed in the direction of the mouse, the girl's eyes went wide with horror.

"*Ewwww!*" she squealed, jumping back and pointing at the mouse. The girls near her stopped what they were doing and looked at the mouse. Two of them ran to the other side of the room. The rest of the class quickly followed as one by one they became aware of the small furry creature. They stood huddled together, hopping up and down unhappily.

"*Mesdemoiselles*, what is the meaning of this outburst?" asked Miss Claudine. "What is going on?"

"A mouse, Miss Claudine," the girls cried.

"What babies!" said Danielle before Miss Claudine could react. "It's more afraid of you than you are of it. I can just chase it right back into its hole."

Danielle ran up to the mouse, which had frozen in its tracks along the baseboard. It did seem frightened, but it didn't head back to its hole. Panicked, it scurried out into the middle of the ballet studio.

"*Aaaahhh!*" The girls screamed and scattered in all directions. The mouse, terrified and confused, ran in circles under their feet.

"*Mesdemoiselles*, please control yourselves," yelled Miss Claudine, clapping her hands for order. "It's just a little mouse."

It was no use. The girls were in a complete panic, shouting and scrambling around the studio. Charlie knew this was her perfect chance. Though she wasn't really afraid of the mouse, she covered her mouth with her hand and began screaming, "A mouse! A mouse!" to blend in with the general commotion.

She inched closer and closer to the door. Then, with one burst of courage, she ran through the doorway into the front room and then straight out the glass front door into the mall.

Charlie kept running until she was almost ten stores away from Miss Claudine's. Finally she had to stop to catch her breath. Clutching her sides, she looked behind her. The mall was now full of shoppers, but no one seemed to be paying any attention to her. No one, that was, except two little boys who gazed at her with bewildered eyes. Charlie realized they were staring because she was dressed in a leotard, tights, and ballet slippers.

The reality of what she had done hit Charlie. She had escaped from Miss Claudine's, but now she was stuck walking around the mall in a ballet outfit. And how on earth was she ever going to find Emma and Lindsey?

# Six

Charlie plopped down wearily on one of the cedar benches that encircled the small decorative pool at the center of the mall. To her left sat an elderly couple who were resting from their morning of shopping. To her right was a woman who had a baby in a stroller, and she was wiping the sticky faces of her little girl and boy.

*This is ridiculous*, thought Charlie, sitting with her chin propped in her hands. *I'll never find them. I never realized Eastbridge Mall was so humongous.*

She had been searching for Emma and Lindsey for almost half an hour with no luck. It seemed to Charlie she had been looking for them for days. Every moment had been torture as she tried to ignore the stares of shoppers who must have wondered why she was walking around the mall in a leotard and ballet slippers.

At first Charlie had concocted a story in her head in which she was a Russian ballet star who had escaped to the United States. She pursed her lips and scowled, hoping her expression conveyed the fact that she had important things on her mind. But one look in a store mirror convinced her that she didn't look a thing like a prima ballerina—not with her red hair pulled back from her face with bobby pins and the slippers that flapped on her feet ever so slightly when she walked.

Then she decided to imagine she was Reva Harris. Reva would have looked so breathtaking in a leotard, and she would have carried herself with such self-assurance, that people would have no choice but to stare at her out of sheer admiration. Charlie tossed her head back saucily and took a deep breath. For a moment the petite ten-year-old disappeared, and a stunning brunette took her place—in Charlie's imagination, at least. She tried to accept the curiosity of the shoppers as proof of their inability to hide their awe at her beauty.

That lasted for about five minutes. Charlie just couldn't convince herself it was true. Every store window reflected the truth back at her. Although she looked perfectly fine as a ten-year-old, she was no Reva Harris.

Charlie slumped down on the bench and wiggled her toes. Her feet were starting to hurt. Ballet slippers obviously weren't built for walking through every single inch of Eastbridge Mall.

She closed her eyes for a moment, and when she opened them—there they were! She saw Emma and Lindsey walking out of Nevins Department Store all the way at the other end of the corridor. They were at least twelve stores away, but there was no mistaking Emma's purple jacket and Lindsey's baby-blue legs.

Charlie jumped up and raced toward them, her ballet slippers slapping the hard cement floor. She couldn't let them get away now that she had found them. As she got closer she could see they were laughing and having a great time.

They stopped to buy a hot dog at a stand outside Nevins. Good, she would be able to catch up to them.

Suddenly Charlie came to a screeching halt. Just three stores away from Nevins was a video arcade, and out of it walked a group of five boys from her class. In the front of the group was Mark Johnson, the only boy Charlie didn't think was a total jerk. In fact, she liked Mark and thought he was cute. He reminded her a little of Lance Pembrook, Reva's boyfriend, with his curly black hair and dimpled chin.

The boys were being their usual selves—punching one another and slumping along, their hands shoved in their pockets. Only Mark moved in a way that Charlie thought resembled human behavior.

The problem was—the boys were heading straight for Charlie! She felt her heart race as she was seized with complete panic. It didn't matter if she *should* care whether or not the boys saw her in her leotard. She *did* care and she had to get out of there—fast!

Charlie looked around quickly. To her left was a pizza parlor. It was risky to duck in there. It was completely open, with only striped pillars separating it from the mall. Besides, the boys might be on their way to it.

To her right was a small clothing store called Barb's Boutique. There wasn't much chance of the boys going in there. Ahead of her she saw Emma and Lindsey sitting on a bench, eating their hot dogs. With any luck the boys would pass right by the boutique, and she could still catch up to Emma and Lindsey.

Charlie bolted across the corridor and pushed open the glass door to Barb's Boutique. She hovered at the side of the door, peering out of the corner to see where the boys were going.

*Good*, she thought, *they're walking by me*. But then they stopped right in front of the boutique. Charlie flattened herself against the side of the doorway so they wouldn't see her. One of the boys pointed to the pizzeria. After a brief discussion, which seemed, to Charlie, to take forever, they turned and went inside for some pizza.

*Darn*, Charlie thought angrily. Now she'd have to wait in the boutique until they were done. If she went out, they'd definitely spot her.

"Look at that girl," a voice behind her said. Charlie whirled around and saw a woman with silver hair swept high on top of her head standing with a short saleswoman with bright orange hair and black-rimmed glasses. They were both staring intently at Charlie. She felt like a trapped animal. There was no place to hide and no place to run.

"That girl is just about the same size as my granddaughter," the silver-haired woman said, pointing at Charlie. "How old are you, dear?"

"Ten, last June," Charlie answered, trying to sound casual and calm.

"I knew it," said the woman happily. "Janine is also ten." She walked closer to Charlie and looked her over seriously. "Are ten-year-olds wearing ballet outfits these days?" she asked without a trace of sarcasm. "It's so difficult to keep up with trends when you're my age. Perhaps I should buy Janine a leotard."

"Oh, no, no," Charlie said. "She'd hate that." The woman eyed her, confused. "You see, I take ballet lessons," Charlie explained. "I'm just . . . um . . . um . . . I'm on a break."

Charlie checked over her shoulder. The boys were still sitting at the front table in the pizza parlor.

"Would you mind trying on a few things?" the woman asked. "I'm visiting my daughter and Janine in Chicago this weekend, and I just can't decide what to bring her."

Trying on clothes was the last thing Charlie wanted to do, but if she didn't the saleslady certainly wouldn't let her hang around the store for much longer. "Sure," she replied, forcing herself to smile. "I'd be glad to."

"Just these few things," said the woman, turning and gathering an armload of dresses she had laid out on the counter.

The saleslady took the dresses from her and piled them into Charlie's arms. "The dressing room is to your left, hon," she said, directing Charlie to a tiny cubicle with a blue curtain in front of it.

Charlie staggered under the weight of the dresses. She could barely fit them all into the cramped dressing room. She pulled the first dress on over her leotard. It had puffed sleeves and a yellow pouf skirt with a crinoline that bunched at the waist.

"Raise your arms a bit, dear," the woman said as Charlie walked out of the dressing room. Feeling ridiculous, Charlie raised her arms over her head. "No, somehow it's just not Janine," the woman commented.

Charlie tried on five more dresses. None of them met with the woman's approval. Charlie was getting tired— and bored. She wanted to get out of there.

The sixth outfit Charlie tried on was a long orange-and-black tiger-striped top with matching stretch pants. A

sequined tiger was machine embroidered on the front of the top, with fake green stones for the eyes. The pants and sleeves both hung on Charlie's petite frame. Charlie hoped, for Janine's sake, that the silver-haired woman would hate this horrible outfit as much as she did.

"This is very trendy," the saleslady commented when Charlie appeared in the pantsuit. "Animal prints are hot right now. We'll be glad to alter the sleeves and pants for you."

Charlie wanted to see if the boys were still eating pizza, so she pretended to be modeling the outfit and walked over by the door. A quick peek told her they were gone. She had to get out of there. "I have to go now," she said. "My break is over."

"Oh, couldn't you stay for just a few more outfits?" the woman requested.

Just then the little bell above the door tinkled. A customer was coming into the shop. Charlie looked over to the door and went pale. It was Mrs. Green, her mother's best friend!

Mrs. Green went right to the front counter and began looking over the jewelry in the case. She hadn't seen Charlie, but it wouldn't be long before she did. Charlie couldn't let that happen.

"I'll try on a few more," Charlie whispered to the woman while the saleslady went off to attend to Mrs. Green. "There are some nice outfits on that rack over there," she continued to whisper, pointing to a carousel of girls' clothing behind the woman. "Why don't you pick out a few more?"

"Good idea," the woman whispered back, "but why are we whispering?"

"I'm just a little hoarse all of a sudden," Charlie lied, rubbing her throat.

The woman nodded and turned to look through the rack of dresses. Charlie immediately crouched low behind a display of suede jackets and crept toward the door. In a second she had pulled the door open and was running out into the mall.

"Stop that kid!" she heard the saleslady yell as she raced down the first corridor and slid around the corner on her slick shoes. At that moment she realized that, technically speaking, she had just stolen the ugly tiger pantsuit. Charlie had never stolen a thing in her life, and even if she was ever tempted to, this outfit would be the last thing on earth she would steal.

Charlie ran and ran, without looking back, until her lungs were ready to burst. Ducking behind a directory sign, she finally stopped and peeked back the way she had come. No one was after her. She had escaped.

Charlie held her aching sides as she caught her breath. How had all of this gotten so out of hand? This morning she had been your regular all-American couch potato. Now she was an escapee from ballet class and a fugitive from the law—dressed in a sequined tiger suit.

# Seven

Charlie peered cautiously around the directory sign. She didn't hear any store alarms or see any police with hound dogs hunting for her. The shoppers in the mall were going about their business, none of them paying any attention to her. Apparently the tiger pantsuit, though ugly and too big, was less conspicuous than the baby-blue leotard.

She tried to figure out where Emma and Lindsey might have gone. She could eliminate Nevins from her search, since she knew they had already been there. She also knew they weren't eating somewhere, since they had just had hot dogs.

The next big store closest to Nevins was Horner's. It was the most logical place to look. Rolling up the pant legs and sleeves of her droopy outfit, Charlie headed toward the large department store.

She walked through the automatic sliding glass doors and took a moment to scan the store quickly. Horner's was set up with mirrors everywhere so that it sometimes looked like there were aisles where there weren't any. If you weren't paying attention you could wind up smacking right into your own reflection.

Charlie went up and down every aisle. She tried not to be distracted, but occasionally she stopped to examine a case of brightly colored watches or to try on a pair of sunglasses. Then she scolded herself for wasting time and moved on.

Frustrated, Charlie tried to focus. She looked up the aisle, and what she saw made her panic. A security guard in a navy-blue uniform was heading straight for her. Maybe he had been alerted to look for the pantsuit thief.

She wasn't sure if he had spotted her or not, but she quickly ducked down behind the nearest rack of men's sport coats and waited for him to pass.

The guard stopped right in front of the coats and looked around. He was young; Charlie guessed he was only about nineteen or twenty. He had short blond hair, steely blue eyes, and a look of serious determination.

Charlie ducked down even lower as the guard was joined by another security guard—a tall, thin woman with a walkie-talkie in her hand. "How's it going today, Daryl?" The woman addressed the other guard pleasantly.

"Fine, thanks, Johnson," Daryl answered, all business. "I've already nabbed two teenage shoplifters this morning."

"You're really on a roll there," the woman commented, with just a hint of laughter in her voice. "Looks like you're trying for the Security Guard of the Month Award. How many collars have you made this week?"

"Exactly fifteen," Daryl answered proudly. "These kids think they can break the law and not get caught. Well, those days are over. I'm going to watch every kid in this store like a hawk."

Daryl walked off briskly. The woman looked after him, smiled, and shook her head, then headed off in the opposite direction.

Charlie breathed for what seemed like the first time since she had seen the guard coming toward her. Just her luck, she was wandering around in a stolen outfit in a store that had an obsessed security guard.

When she was sure Daryl was gone, she crept out from behind the coats and made her way up the escalator. She let it carry her along, not exactly sure where she should look next. She had just about given up on ever finding Emma and Lindsey.

She got off the escalator on the second floor—and there they were! Emma and Lindsey were standing at the Madame Lacroix makeup counter, dabbing their fingers in the pots of eyeshadow powder and streaking them onto their lids.

Charlie didn't know how to approach them. She was afraid they would run away when they saw her. She decided it was best to act casual.

"Hi, you guys," she said breezily, as if she had just happened to run into them. Emma and Lindsey whirled around and faced her with trapped, guilty expressions.

"What are you doing here?" Emma demanded. "You're supposed to be in ballet class."

"*I'm* supposed to be in ballet class?" Charlie shrieked. Then, not wanting to make a scene, she lowered her voice to a whisper. "What about the two of you? You're supposed to be in ballet class, too."

"That's our business," Emma said huffily.

"How'd you get out?" Lindsey asked.

Charlie told them the mouse story. " . . . and then when everyone was screaming, I just ducked out," she concluded.

"Neat," Emma said, admiring Charlie's quick thinking. "Maybe you're not as big a twerp as I thought you were."

"Thanks loads," Charlie snapped.

"I can't say I love your outfit, though," Emma added. "Did you just buy it?"

"How could I buy anything?" Charlie demanded. "My wallet, my clothes, everything's back at Miss Claudine's."

"Then how'd you wind up in that weird getup?" Lindsey wanted to know.

Charlie told them *that* story. "What a riot," Emma said, laughing. "At least you saved poor Janine from getting that ugly thing for a present."

"I guess I'll mail it back to the boutique or something," Charlie said. "It's better than walking around in a leotard."

"Not much." Emma wrinkled up her nose as she looked at the outfit.

"You've really been busy," Lindsey commented, impressed with Charlie's adventures. "We've just been wandering around, looking at things and trying stuff on."

"I can see that," said Charlie, studying their makeup-smeared faces. Emma was now wearing five different-colored stripes of eye makeup. Her cheeks were smudged with three stripes of badly blended blush, and she had silver sparkly powder all over her forehead.

The makeup looked even more strange on Lindsey. The entire area under one eyebrow was completely green, the other eye area was covered in bright blue. She wore a purplish lipstick on her top lip and a reddish-brown color on the bottom.

"It's good that you're here," Emma said cheerfully.

"We've run out of face space for trying on makeup. Your face is like a blank piece of paper to draw on."

Charlie didn't know what to say. She didn't want to wind up looking like Emma and Lindsey. Still, she was surprised to discover how glad she was that they were finally being nice to her. Now that they were all in trouble together, it seemed as if they were united by a special bond. And after everything she had just been through, it felt good to have friendly faces around her.

"Come on over here," Emma said, taking Charlie by the arm. "Madame Lacroix is really for old ladies. They don't have any good colors." She pulled Charlie over to a counter with a sign that said *Dazzlers*.

"Besides," Lindsey added in a confidential tone, "we have to keep moving from counter to counter before the salesladies yell at us. They don't really like you using the samples once they figure out that you're not going to buy anything."

Emma stood Charlie in front of the mirror on the counter. "You have sort of hazel eyes, so I think we'll start with some green eyeshadow," she said, picking up a thick crayonlike stick of green makeup with gold flecks running through it. "Now close your eyes."

Charlie let Emma draw lines in the creases of her lids and then smudge them with strong, confident fingers. "Wow," she said when she opened her eyes and examined her face in the mirror. "It looks kind of good."

"You need mascara and highlight color," Emma commented, studying her face.

"How did you get to know so much about makeup?"

Charlie asked as Emma smeared a gold creamy shadow under her eyebrows.

"I'm going to be an artist when I'm older," Emma explained. "Putting on makeup is just like painting, only you do it on a face instead of on paper. It's really just knowing how to blend color and shadow and highlights. I learned all about that stuff when I took painting classes after school last year."

"I'll never be good at putting on makeup," said Lindsey, leaning up against the counter and watching Emma work on Charlie's face. "I'm not sure what I want to be when I'm older. I learned to ski last winter, and I thought about being an Olympic skier. But that's not really a job."

"You could be a ski instructor," Charlie suggested, studying her made-up eyes in the mirror.

"Maybe," agreed Lindsey. "What do you want to be?"

"I'm not totally sure," Charlie said as Emma blended a pink cream blush into her cheeks. "I just know I want to be on TV. I guess that means I want to be an actress. But maybe I could be a TV reporter, or a game-show host. I don't really care, just as long as it has to do with TV."

"I'll tell you what I don't want to be," said Emma. "I don't want to be a ballerina."

"That's for sure," agreed Lindsey. "What kind of stuff did they do after we left?"

"We did something that sounds like 'Arabs,'" Charlie told her. "We had to stand on one foot. It was dumb."

"Do you mean arabesques?" Emma asked.

"I think so," Charlie said. "I guess you already know all this stuff."

"Some of it," Emma muttered. "Now you need some lipstick," she added, surveying the different colors that were set out in little sample tubes. "I think a goldish color would be good for you."

"What gets me," said Lindsey, "is that everybody else seems to already know the stuff. Miss Claudine just expected us to figure it all out. How can we know it if no one explains it to us?"

"You do sort of pick it up," Emma said, dabbing one color onto Charlie's lips and then rubbing it off. "Way too orange," she decided. "And Miss Claudine would eventually come around and start twisting your body into the right positions. Somehow you just get the hang of it."

"Were you good at ballet?" Charlie managed to mumble while Emma applied another color lipstick.

"Naw," Emma admitted. "I stank. My last teacher said I wasn't trying. She was right, I wasn't."

"I think I would stink even if I tried," Charlie confessed miserably. "I was trying to do the Arab thing and I stank. I'm terrible at anything that has to do with moving around. Moving is my worst thing."

"That's all in your head," Lindsey argued. "Nobody's bad at moving."

"I am," Charlie insisted. "You'd probably be good at it, since you're athletic."

"No way," said Lindsey, as if the suggestion that she might be good at ballet was an insult. "Ballet is totally different. It's so . . . so frilly."

"You do have a fabulous *port de bras*," Emma teased.

Lindsey quickly crossed her arms defensively. Charlie

and Emma looked at her scowling face and started to giggle. As Lindsey got the joke, her frown slowly cracked into a smile, and she joined their laughter.

Charlie was the first to stop laughing. She had spotted Daryl, the security guard, heading their way. This time there was no mistake. His steely eyes were staring right at them.

"We'd better get out of here," said Charlie, nodding toward the approaching guard.

"We're not doing anything," Emma protested.

"That guy hates kids," Charlie explained quickly. "He'll call our parents even if we're innocent. Besides, I'm wearing this sort-of-stolen clothing."

"You'd better tuck in those tags," Emma said, eyeing the two tags hanging from Charlie's wrists. "They're a dead giveaway, don't you think?"

"Shoot," whispered Charlie, frantically stuffing the tags up her sleeves.

"Hey, you kids," the guard shouted. "Don't move!"

The girls froze for a second, then, without further discussion, they turned and raced down the aisle.

"Stop!" called the guard, running after them.

"Maybe we *should* stop," said Charlie as they careened around the side of a scarf counter.

"Forget it," panted Emma. "Do you want your mother to have to pick you up at the security office?"

"I thought you didn't care about getting into trouble," Lindsey reminded Emma.

Emma shot Lindsey an annoyed look. "Just be quiet and keep running!" she ordered. "He's getting closer!"

# Eight

Charlie, Emma, and Lindsey crouched low as they hurried along the scarf counter. They'd given the security guard the slip—for the moment. He stood in the aisle, looking for them.

"Now what?" Lindsey turned to Emma and demanded.

"How should I know?" Emma hissed back as she ventured a peek over the top of the counter.

"Keep your head down!" Charlie snapped. "He'll see you."

"Well, we can't stay here forever," Emma reminded her needlessly. "I have to see if the coast is clear, don't I?"

The security guard was now standing absolutely still, like a wild animal sniffing the air for the scent of its prey. His blue eyes narrowed as he surveyed the rows of merchandise, looking for anything unusual.

"That guy gives me the creeps," commented Charlie fearfully.

"Yeah," Lindsey agreed. "He has this never-give-up quality. I can imagine him still looking for us when we're seventy-five."

"Shhhh," Emma silenced them. "He won't have to look much longer if you two keep blabbing."

At that moment the guard seemed to sense their presence and headed down the aisle toward them.

"Let's go," whispered Lindsey. The three girls kept low and scooted across the aisle.

"I said stop," yelled the guard, catching sight of them. "Stop this minute!"

In seconds the girls were running pell-mell down the aisle, weaving paths through the shoppers. Daryl broke into a run and was quickly right behind them.

The girls' hearts raced. They knew it was only a matter of seconds before he nabbed one of them. Yet they seemed to be getting away.

A quick check over her shoulder told Charlie what had happened. Two teenage boys wearing gray Horner's stockroom jackets had wheeled a long rack full of fur coats across the aisle, blocking the guard's path. One boy had stopped to tie his shoelace. "Move that thing!" Charlie heard the guard shout.

"Hold your horses," the boy snapped back.

Charlie knew this was their lucky break, but they had to act fast. "I don't think we can outrun him," she said, breathing hard. "Let's find someplace to hide."

The girls quickly ducked behind a rack of ladies' nightgowns in the lingerie department. "There's a dressing room over there," Emma told Charlie and Lindsey. Unable to come up with a better plan, the two girls followed as Emma scrambled toward the ladies' dressing room.

"Grab something so you look like you're trying it on," Emma instructed them.

"Like what?" asked Lindsey, looking around at the rows of fancy lacy lingerie.

"Like anything," Emma said, quickly handing Lindsey

a frilly slip and Charlie a bra on a plastic hanger. She took a purple-flowered nightgown for herself. "Just get into that dressing room."

The woman at the entrance of the dressing room eyed them suspiciously but gave them each a ticket marked *One Item.* "I don't think that will fit you," she said, looking at the black underwire bra Charlie carried in her hand. "I doubt you're a C-cup."

"Oh, you'd be surprised," Charlie said coolly, a little shocked by her own boldness.

The woman rolled her eyes and shook her head wearily but let her pass. Once inside the dressing room, the girls made their way down the single long, narrow aisle lined with individual stalls. They looked at the feet under the louvered doors until they found one stall at the very end that was empty.

"Now what do we do?" Lindsey asked.

"Stop asking that," Emma snapped.

"For someone who said she doesn't care about getting in trouble, you sure seem nervous," Lindsey challenged.

"I meant I don't care about getting into trouble with my mother, or the principal, or someone like that. I've never been in trouble with the police before."

"He isn't really a policeman," said Charlie. "He's just a store guard."

"Close enough for me," Emma replied, leaning against the wall. "The only thing to do now is wait in here and hope we've lost him."

The girls slid down the wall of the dressing room and sat in a row on the floor, opposite the full-length mirror.

They sat in silence for several minutes, staring at their reflections. "You know, we do look pretty weird," Lindsey said finally. "How come I have a different-colored eyeshadow on each eye?"

"Because the saleslady in the makeup department at Nevins chased us away from the counter before I could finish making up your other eye, remember?" Emma reminded her.

"Oh, yeah," Lindsey recalled. "Charlie's makeup looks nice."

"But you're not wearing this stupid outfit," Charlie said.

"Why don't you take it off?" Lindsey suggested. "It makes you kind of easy to spot."

"I have to return it somehow," Charlie explained. "Besides, we'd stand out anyway with all this makeup on and the two of us in matching blue tights."

"I can't believe you told that woman you could fit into that bra." Emma giggled.

Charlie laughed at the memory. "What else was I supposed to say? You're the one who handed it to me." She held the bra up in front of her. "It's strange to think that someday maybe I *will* fit into this."

"I can't picture myself with a woman's body, can you?" asked Lindsey seriously.

"I definitely can," Emma answered. "I want to be nice and slim."

Charlie got to her feet and took the bra off the hanger. She wiggled her arms out of the sleeves of the tiger top and put the bra on over her leotard. Then she slipped her arms back in and stood with her hands on her hips in front of Emma and Lindsey. The stiff underwire in the bra gave her a full shape. "This is what I'll probably look like."

Emma and Lindsey broke into gales of laughter at the ridiculous sight. "You're *too* strange," panted Emma with a note of admiration in her voice. Lindsey was too convulsed with laughter to say anything.

Suddenly, Emma held up her hand for quiet. "Shhhh, listen," she ordered them sharply.

Sure enough, they heard the unmistakable sound of the security guard's voice, but they couldn't quite make out what he was saying. Emma slowly cracked the stall door a half inch, and the girls crowded together, trying to pick up the guard's words.

"I just came on duty, and I don't know who's in there," they heard a woman at the door tell the guard. From the sound of her voice they could tell that she wasn't the same woman who had let them in. "You can't go in there," the woman insisted.

"Either you check for me or I'm going in," the guard replied.

Lindsey looked at Charlie in horror. "It would be easier to escape a pack of bloodhounds," she whispered.

"I can't go in until I get someone to relieve me at the door here," the woman argued.

"We have to get out of here now," Emma breathed frantically.

"But he's standing right outside," Lindsey pointed out. "Face it, we're goners. We're trapped."

They could tell from the tone of his voice that the guard was angry with the woman at the door. They were arguing in low tones, then the guard raised his voice. "All right," he snapped. "I'll be back with a saleswoman."

Without further discussion, the girls slipped out of the stall and made their way toward the front of the narrow dressing room with their backs pressed against the stall doors.

They huddled together near the inside of the entrance. The woman was sitting on a high stool, leafing through the pages of a magazine. The girls exchanged worried glances, and then Lindsey dropped to her hands and knees and began crawling silently out the door. The other two got onto their knees, as well.

Emma and Charlie watched as Lindsey made it safely around the corner of the partition separating the entrance of the dressing room from the rest of the store. The woman never looked up from her magazine. Emma scrambled out next. She, too, rounded the partition safely.

Charlie sucked in her breath and began crawling with her head down. She didn't dare to breathe or even look up at the woman. She just crawled and crawled—and suddenly stopped right under the woman's feet! She couldn't go any farther; her pant leg was caught on a carpet staple that was sticking up from the floor.

With trembling hands, Charlie reached back and worked the cloth free from the staple. Some instinct made her look up quickly, and her eyes met those of the saleslady, which were boring down on her.

Charlie jumped to her feet and faced the woman. Before either of them could speak, the guard approached with the saleswoman who had originally let them into the dressing room.

"There's one of them now," yelled the guard, catching sight of Charlie.

"And she's stealing a bra!" added the saleswoman with him. "She didn't have that chest when she came in."

Charlie's eyes darted down to her chest, and to her horror she realized she was still wearing the underwire bra she had put on as a joke back in the dressing room.

The saleswoman at the doorway reached out and grabbed her arm. That was enough to snap Charlie out of her state of frozen terror. She yanked her arm away and darted across the lingerie department.

"This way," whispered a voice at her side. It was Emma. She and Lindsey had been waiting for Charlie, crouched low at the far side of the hosiery counter. Charlie took off with them and heard the guard yelling, "Stop!" as he chased them once again.

Emma led them into a crowd of people waiting at the elevator bank. Just as they got there, a door opened. "Excuse me, excuse me," they mumbled as they wriggled and pushed their way to the front of the crowd and onto the elevator. They ran to the back of the car and flattened themselves against the wall as the throng of shoppers packed in behind them.

The security guard screeched to a stop in front of the elevator door as it began to close. Looking over heads and under legs he searched for them. They weren't sure if he saw them or not, but in seconds the door closed and they were on their way to the upper floors of the store.

Charlie leaned back against the wall with her eyes shut, panting. "This is like a nightmare," she whispered.

"Shhhh," whispered Emma. "We'll get off at the third floor. I have an idea."

The third was the top floor. There was a restaurant and a restroom just outside the elevator. The girls headed for the ladies' room.

"Thanks for waiting," Charlie said as she plopped down on a chair in the front powder room.

"No problem," Lindsey assured her. "We're in this mess together." She looked at Charlie and added, "I think you'd better take that thing off."

"Oh, this stupid thing," Charlie muttered as she wiggled out of the bra. "I keep getting accused of stealing all this stuff I don't even want!"

"Listen, this is my plan," said Emma. "We find the fire stairs and take them down to the bottom floor. We've just got to get out of this store."

"Good idea," Lindsey agreed. "Let's go."

Trying to look calm and casual, the girls walked out of the ladies' room. Charlie hung the bra on the arm of the first mannequin she saw.

They followed the walls until they came to a sign marked *Fire Exit—Use in Emergency Only*. They ducked into the stairwell and made their way down the three flights of stairs.

They stopped on the first floor. "Just act cool and head straight for the first exit you see," Emma instructed them. "Once we're back out in the mall we'll get as far away from Horner's as we can."

"That will bring us back to Miss Claudine's," Lindsey objected.

"Don't worry about that now," Emma said. "Let's just get out of here."

Charlie cracked open the door and looked around. "The nearest exit is straight through the pet department on the left," she reported. "Follow me."

The girls headed for the pet department. They stepped through the archway that led into the aisles full of adorable kittens and puppies. The entrance to the mall was just yards away, past the large cages filled with tiny yellow canaries.

"Almost there," Lindsey whispered encouragingly.

Suddenly an all-too-familiar voice resounded in their ears. "Stop those kids!" Daryl the security guard raced toward them from the other end of the first floor.

"Go!" yelled Lindsey.

# Nine

The exit was so near, but Daryl was closing in on them with lightning speed. Lindsey bounded out the door, and Emma was right behind her. Charlie would have been third if the cuff of her pants hadn't chosen that moment to come unrolled and trip her up.

"Darn!" she cried as she reached out for something to break her fall. Her fingers clutched the strong gold wires of a large canary cage, and she brought it crashing down to the ground as she fell.

The air was immediately full of chirping yellow birds. The impact of the fall had sprung the catch of the cage door, freeing the canaries.

"Young lady!" cried a salesman, running out from behind the counter. "Look what you've done!"

Charlie looked up at him with frightened eyes. How was she going to explain to her mother that even though she had run away from ballet class, stolen a pantsuit and a bra, and freed all the canaries in the pet department—none of it was her fault? She would have to think of something, because this certainly had to be the end of the line for her.

But just as the salesman was about to grab her, he collided with the guard, who was running toward her from the opposite direction. They hit with a slam, bouncing off one another and into the rabbit cages on one side and the snake tanks on the other.

Charlie saw her opportunity and took it. In a split second she was up and out the door. This time there was no sign of Emma and Lindsey.

Charlie turned sharply to her left and kept running. A *pssst* sound made her stop and look around. "Over here!" It was Lindsey and Emma waving to her from the covered entrance of a men's clothing store. Long glass showcases with mannequins in suits shielded them on either side.

"I can't believe you got away again," said Emma.

"Me, neither," Charlie agreed. "Now what do we do?"

The girls scanned the mall in front of them. Sure enough, Daryl was heading toward them, looking furious. Besides the stores, the only other thing near them was a small trailer with a low wooden stage in front of it. A sign read: *Eastbridge Mall Annual Talent Contest at 12:30 PM*. People were already starting to sit on the metal folding chairs that were set up in front of the stage.

Reading the sign made Charlie suddenly think about time. "Gosh, what time is it?" she asked.

Emma and Lindsey shrugged. "Wait a minute, I think there's a clock inside this store," Lindsey said, holding her hands up to her eyes and peering through the glass door. "It's twelve-fifteen," she reported.

"Listen, I have a plan," said Emma seriously. "We'll walk casually over to that talent show and mingle with the crowd. Then we'll make our way to the side of the trailer, and when the coast is clear, we'll run out to the parking lot and wait for Charlie's mother."

"But all our clothes are back at Miss Claudine's," Lindsey objected.

Emma thought for a moment. "I don't know, say that you forgot them. I can't think of everything!"

"We'll say Miss Claudine is such a nut that she locked us out without our clothes," Charlie suggested. "We'll tell my mother that only Emma was able to grab her things before Miss Claudine went on a wild rampage and threw everyone out of the studio. She won't let us go back if she thinks Miss Claudine is a total nutcase."

"Brilliant," said Emma. "I really misjudged you, Charlie. I thought you were just a goody-goody."

"Well, you're not as weird as I thought," Charlie admitted.

"What about me?" asked Lindsey. "What did you guys think of me?"

"Jock," Emma and Charlie answered at once.

"Is that bad?" asked Lindsey, bewildered. "I *am* a jock."

"Sometimes it's annoying," Charlie said, "but you're an okay jock."

"Yeah," Emma agreed, "At least you're not the bossy, loudmouthed kind. If I had to be on a team, I'd be on yours."

Lindsey beamed. "Thanks. You guys are okay, too."

The three girls smiled at one another, then Emma grew serious. "It's good we all like each other, because we might end up as cellmates in jail if that guard finds us. There's a pretty good crowd over there. Let's go."

They peeked around the corner of the glass showcase. Daryl had walked past them and was at the end of the mall corridor. He was about to circle back up their way.

"Keep your head down and walk slowly," Emma instructed as they started across the corridor.

Wordlessly, the girls made their way through the crowd toward the trailer. The guard was now standing in front of the metal chairs, looking all around.

Just as they were about to slip past the trailer, a woman with curly white hair popped her head out of its side door and called to them. "Hurry, girls," she called. "The dog act ahead of you hasn't shown up. I need you to go on first."

The girls looked at one another. The woman had obviously mistaken them for some other kids. "We're not—" Lindsey began to explain, but a quick poke from Emma stopped her. The guard was walking up the center aisle between the chairs. He hadn't seen them, but in a minute he would.

"No problem," said Charlie as the three of them quickly stepped up into the trailer. Inside, the place was crowded with people, most of them teenagers and kids, practicing their acts. There was a small boy with a wooden dummy on his lap, a teenage girl with a French horn, small twin girls in tuxedoes and tap shoes, a rap group dressed in red nylon jackets, a tall, thin boy with a guitar, and assorted other people either dressing or rehearsing.

A girl of about twelve who was holding a flute came over to them. "You must be the Tip Toe Dancers," she said, looking them over icily. "I heard you were the act to beat, but you don't look so hot to me."

"Then obviously you don't see too well," Charlie hissed back. "We're the greatest."

"Hmmmph," the girl said, turning on her heel and storming away.

"This is crazy!" whispered Lindsey. "Every time we turn around we're in an even bigger mess than we were before!"

"Would you rather go out there and get caught?" asked Emma, hands on hips.

"We'd better come up with an act," Charlie reminded them. "The Tip Toe Dancers are now on first. I can see why that woman thought we were in the show. We have all this makeup on and everything."

"Take off that tiger suit," said Emma, taking off her own jacket. "I still have my leotard on under my clothes. At least we'll have matching costumes. Lindsey, you take off your T-shirt."

"No way," Lindsey argued.

"Lindsey, this is an emergency," Charlie coaxed as she pulled the tiger top over her head. "You look fine in the leotard. Honestly, you do."

"Oh, all right," Lindsey agreed, pulling the shirt over her head sullenly. In a minute the girls stood in their blue leotards, clutching their clothes.

"What are we going to do once we get onstage?" asked Lindsey.

"Dance on our tiptoes, I guess," Emma said with a shrug of her shoulders. "I wonder what happened to the real Tip Toe Dancers?"

"It's showtime, ladies," said the white-haired woman, ushering the three girls to the main trailer door that led out onto the wooden stage. "Mr. Johnson has the tape you sent all set to go."

"G-g-great," Charlie stammered, smiling feebly at the woman.

The girls stood in the doorway just as a man onstage announced to the audience, "Please welcome our first act, the Tip Toe Dancers."

There was a polite ripple of applause. The girls stood stock still in the doorway, still holding their clothing, frozen with stage fright. "Come on, now," the woman encouraged, giving each of them a gentle push onto the stage, "give them your best."

Dropping their clothing in a pile at the side of the stage, the girls stood and listened to the music. Charlie recognized it as a piece from *The Nutcracker*, a ballet score that her mother sometimes liked to listen to while she cleaned the house.

Charlie knew they couldn't just stand there. *Pretend you're on TV*, she told herself, and she began doing an arabesque, just as she had learned at Miss Claudine's. To her surprise, she was able to keep her balance.

Emma knew the move from her previous classes and imitated Charlie. Lindsey did the same. With their legs extended behind them, the three girls began hopping in a circle.

Emma then broke out of the circle and began spinning around the stage with her arms over her head. Lindsey and Charlie did the same. They were surprised at how the music carried them along. Soon they were leaping across the stage and kicking their legs out in front, throwing their arms wide to either side. The music was so lively they simply had to jump around joyfully.

Occasionally the girls smacked into one another, but they just went right on dancing. The audience seemed to

assume that they were a comedy act and laughed and clapped along with them.

Every so often they glanced out into the crowd. Daryl, the guard, was standing in front of the stage, but he wasn't paying any attention to them, even as they danced right before his very eyes. He was looking for three girls who were dressed differently and who most certainly were not performing in a talent contest—or so he thought.

"I wish he'd go away," Charlie whispered to Emma as she twirled past.

"Just keep dancing," Emma muttered back, smiling to the audience as she spun by.

As Charlie turned around she noticed three girls just about their age standing in the trailer doorway, wearing gauzy pink tutus and angry expressions. They were clearly the real Tip Toe Dancers.

Charlie and Lindsey looked at Emma with wide, panicked eyes. Emma just kept smiling at the audience, leaping and twirling. She took her friends' hands and danced them into a circle.

They turned out from their circle just in time to see the guard shrug his shoulders and walk away slowly. They had escaped!

Not wasting a second, Emma danced over to the pile of clothing and scooped up her things gracefully. Charlie and Lindsey did the same. Emma then danced down the wooden stairs at the center of the stage, with Charlie and Lindsey right behind her.

The audience laughed and clapped as the girls twirled the rest of the way out into the mall.

# Ten

Charlie, Emma, and Lindsey stopped twirling and broke into a run. They weren't sure which way they were headed. All they knew was that this was their chance to get far away from that side of the mall.

When Charlie ran past the boutique where she had tried on the tiger suit, she kept her head down. Then, summoning her courage, she ran back to the store, threw the outfit in the door, and raced after Emma and Lindsey. It felt great to be free at last of the ugly "stolen" outfit.

The three girls ran down the ramp to the lower level of the mall, and before they knew it, they were in the corridor that led to Miss Claudine's. "We made it," panted Lindsey.

Oddly enough, Charlie and Emma knew what she meant. Miss Claudine's did seem like a friendly place somehow. Certainly no one here had chased them—and Miss Claudine had actually been pretty nice to them.

They stood in front of the ballet school and looked at one another. Emma peered through the glass pane in the front door. She could see into half the studio. "This must be the 'ballet culture' part. It looks like they're all just sitting around on the floor, and Miss Claudine is telling them something," she reported. "What do you think we should do?"

"I'm tired of running and making up stories," Charlie

said. "I just want to go inside and finish up the class. If she tells my mother, then she tells her. I don't even care anymore."

"Me, too," said Lindsey. "At least we're not sitting in some store security office or anything."

"Okay," agreed Emma skeptically. "Let's go."

They opened the front door as quietly as they could. Immediately they heard the pleasant sound of Miss Claudine's voice. " . . . and so, *chéries*, though much of *Swan Lake* is very sad, in the end, the evil Rothbart's spell is broken, and Prince Siegfried and his beloved swan princess are united in the kingdom under the sea— together at last."

One by one, Charlie, then Emma, then Lindsey, slipped into the studio and sat at the back of the group of girls. This time Miss Claudine clearly saw them, but she didn't say anything. She simply continued with her explanation of *Swan Lake*. "The end of this ballet is so beautiful that the entire audience weeps. The swans lie gracefully on the stage as we see Siegfried and Odette sail off in a magical boat." Miss Claudine's blue eyes seemed to mist up at the very memory of the scene.

Charlie, Emma, and Lindsey looked at the faces of the other girls. They, too, seemed moved by the story. It made them wish they had been there to hear the whole thing.

"*Swan Lake* has some of the most beautiful chorus work ever seen," Miss Claudine continued. "The dancers must move together as if they were almost one body. It's fine to be a star on your own, but before you can be that, you must be able to work as part of a group."

The girls weren't sure, but they suspected that Miss Claudine was directing the next part of her speech at them. "That is why I never force a student. Each person must be moved by the music and her own inner spirit. Either you choose companionship with other dancers and a love for ballet, or you do not."

Charlie wasn't sure about her love for ballet, yet when she'd been dancing on the stage, as goofy as it had looked, she had been swept up by the music. She'd felt free and happy.

Emma drew imaginary circles on the wood floor as Miss Claudine continued to talk about the love of ballet. It struck her that the teacher really believed what she was saying. Being near someone so passionate about the subject sort of changed her attitude about ballet.

Lindsey, too, was struck by Miss Claudine's remarks, but in a different way. She loved teamwork. She'd never realized there was so much of it involved with ballet.

"Go now, *mesdemoiselles*," Miss Claudine concluded. "Hold the image of yourselves as beautiful swans in your heads until I see you all again on Wednesday. *Au revoir*."

Charlie, Emma, and Lindsey jumped up and ran for the dressing room, relieved that Miss Claudine hadn't scolded them. They put on their clothes and washed the makeup off their faces in the bathroom.

"It's like she doesn't care whether we're here or not," commented Emma, sounding almost hurt. "I don't even know if she knew we were gone."

"She knew," Lindsey said. "I guess it's like she said, she doesn't force anybody to do anything."

**Miss Claudine's**

SCHOOL OF BALLET

"That's almost unnatural, coming from an adult," Charlie commented.

"I'll say," Emma agreed.

"It's like being treated as an adult," Lindsey said. The girls thought about that for a minute. It was strange and unfamiliar, but they liked the idea.

As the three of them headed for the door, older students were coming in. There were boys as well as girls in this class. They looked graceful and confident to the younger girls.

A few moments later, the three friends stood in front of Miss Claudine's waiting for Charlie's mother to pick them up. "Will you guys be going on Wednesday?" Charlie asked.

"I don't know," answered Emma. "Are you going?"

"I'll probably have to," Charlie replied.

"It's not really that bad," Lindsey said. "Besides, we have each other for company."

Slowly, a smile spread across each girl's face. "It's true," said Charlie, "we do have each other."

The girls looked at one another and started to laugh. The whole morning's events suddenly struck them as very funny.

"You girls certainly seem to have had a good time," said Mrs. Clark happily as she approached them. "I told you you'd like ballet. What did you do on your first day?"

"Ummm, not much," Charlie answered with a mischievous smile. "We all just sort of got to know one another."